# DEPUTY JENNINGS
# MEETS THE AMISH

*a novella by* **Jim Potter**

sandhenge
PUBLICATIONS

*Deputy Jennings Meets the Amish*
By Jim Potter

This is a work of fiction. Names, characters, places, and incidents are either the product of the author's imagination or are used fictitiously. Any resemblance to actual persons, living or dead, events or locales, is entirely coincidental. If you want legal advice, hire an attorney. If you're seeking medical guidance, see a doctor. For thought-provoking entertainment, keep reading.

Cover design by Gina Laiso, Integrita Productions
Interior design by Gina Laiso, Integrita Productions
Sculptures, including *Tom Jennings* on cover, by J. Alex Potter

Potter, Jim, 1949-
Deputy Jennings meets the Amish
Sandhenge Publications, 2022
Hutchinson, KS

Library of Congress Control Number: 2022905348
ISBN-13: 9780979069727 (perfect bound)
ISBN-13: 9780979069734 (e-book)
FICTION / Literary. FICTION 1. Amish 2. Police 3. Culture

Printed in the United States
First Edition

Also, by the author:

*Taking Back the Bullet: Trajectories of Self-Discovery*
*Cop in the Classroom: Lessons I've Learned, Tales I've Told*
*Under the Radar: Race at School (a play)*

*To wisdom*

*"Wisdom begins
when you realize
there are other
points of view."*
-Origin unknown

# Acknowledgments

I acknowledge my parents, Harold, and Nell Potter, for instilling in me the importance of learning and education.

This novella didn't happen in a vacuum. I'm fortunate to live in an environment with J. Alex Potter—artist, partner, and first reader—where we prioritize space that gives life to our inspirations.

Thanks to Marilyn Bolton for her "fresh eyes" in reading my manuscript.

Would a book be a book without a cover? If it weren't for Gina Laiso, Integrita Productions, the front cover would have been a simple horse-and-buggy warning sign. Instead, Gina created a dynamic image, continuing the theme of Tom Jennings encountering challenges while working patrol.

Finally, I thank the members of the Old Order Amish community who live in Reno County, Kansas. During my days working for the Reno County Sheriff's Office as a patrol officer, and later as a school resource officer, I had the good fortune of interacting with people of the Amish faith.

*Deputy Jennings Meets the Amish* is a work of fiction. None of my characters are real people, but they're real to me, and I hope they're real to you.

Jim Potter
Greater Medora

# Preface

A friend of mine shared one of her concerns by posting it on *Facebook*. Here's a portion of that communication:

"The ditches are being dug out along the county road by our house, and I'm seeing many loads of soil trucked away to who-knows-where. Things like this should probably not bother me, but I feel sorry for the farmers of the adjacent fields who lost all that topsoil and will never see it again."

After additional interactive posts by other people about erosion, who owns the topsoil, and questions about if it would be against the law for a farmer to recover the soil, I started a fictional story.

# Contents

# 1

# Deputy Tom Jennings
# Meets Rosanna Yoder

"How can this be happening to me?" thought Rosanna.

Earlier, Adam, her husband, had remarked, "We sure had a gully washer overnight!"

"How are my flowers?" she had asked, concerned about filling business orders prior to the upcoming holiday.

"Those in bloom took a beating, but the others may come around with a break in the weather," Adam had replied. He added, "The fierce storm has done more than damage your flowers; a corner of the garden has flowed into the ditch.

Adam had left for town on the tractor, pulling their horse trailer, taking pigs and chickens to the sale barn in Prairie Grove.

As soon as he departed, Rosanna got to work. She knew how to use a shovel and a wheelbarrow, and she had the muscles to prove it. After checking her flowers, Rosanna started collecting the garden's rich topsoil from the county ditch. With each trip of heavy wet soil, she strained to control the wheelbarrow, especially when the wheel slid off the board path that she had laid down on the saturated ground.

On every wheelbarrow trip, Rosanna promised herself that she would plant additional grass to prevent damaging erosion from future gully washers. As she turned back towards the ditch, she saw a county patrol car slowing down with its turn signal blinking, indicating the vehicle was preparing to enter her driveway. The side of the vehicle identified it as a "K-9 Unit." Rosanna ignored the driver but observed the dog in the rear seat, a German shepherd.

She touched her right cheek.

Rosanna remembered growing up with occasional brief visits from deputy sheriffs. Her mouth dry, she wet her lips and swallowed, praying that God's will would include a safe Adam, one who hadn't been in an accident. Then she considered her husband's family in Pennsylvania. Had there been a death? Was the deputy here for a death notification? She almost laughed. Those days were over. Access to cell phones had changed their world.

\*

The deputy was an extra-large man with a bald head and a ready smile. His grin revealed a lot. Rosanna figured he wasn't the bearer of bad news.

The obese officer struggled to dislodge himself from his car. For a minute, it appeared the steering wheel and safety belt would prevent him from ever exiting his vehicle. Winded, he finally pulled himself out. The canine stared at her and lifted his nose toward the partially open side-window.

"Hello ma'am, I'm Deputy Tom Jennings with the Cottonwood County Sheriff's Office."

Rosanna bit her lip and replied, "Hello, sir, I'm Rosanna Yoder with the Old Order Amish."

"Nice to meet you. Looks like you've got some work ahead of you," said Jennings, observing the nearby mudslide.

Rosanna nodded but waited to learn why law enforcement was visiting her.

"I'm here because I'm responding to a 911 call," said Jennings. "A county employee called the dispatcher and told her that there was a theft in progress, that someone was stealing dirt from this location."

"I haven't seen anyone stealing dirt around here," replied Rosanna. "Did the dispatcher get a description of the vehicle?" she asked.

"The description was an attractive Amish woman wearing a dark-blue dress."

"Oh!" exclaimed Rosanna. "Me? . . . but I'm not stealing anything," she replied. "May I call my husband? He's in town."

"Yes, sure, but I still need to talk with you. I need more information for my report. Would you like to use my phone?"

\*

Deputy Jennings got his phone out and gave it a command: "Call Miller's Sale Barn, Prairie Grove, Kansas."

A minute later, once her husband was on the phone, Jennings watched as Rosanna Yoder, an Amish woman wearing a dark-blue dress and a white head covering, both decorated with splashes of dried dirt, walked in her muddy tennis shoes towards the enclosed front porch. Jennings waited, already back in his SUV, working on his computerized report.

Rosanna's call to Adam was brief. She explained that a deputy sheriff—polite enough—was questioning her about taking "dirt" out of the ditch. Adam told her there was nothing to worry about; her interaction with the sheriff would not be a problem; it was just a cultural misunderstanding.

"Adam," Rosanna said, ". . . one more thing . . . he's got a police dog with him. It's in the rear seat of the car. It's a German shepherd."

"That's all in the past," Adam assured his wife.

Jennings had better things to do. He knew this was a waste of his time, but he also recognized he couldn't ignore the call, especially from a county employee of the Road and Bridge Department. If the employee was concerned enough to contact the department, then there would most likely be a follow-up call inquiring about how the investigation was handled.

Jennings planned to get answers and return to the road. He didn't want to make a federal case out of this assignment, but he also had to be conscientious about the work. He was trying to cover his big butt from any potential trouble from his psychotic supervisors. He wasn't paranoid, but recently they'd been nitpicking his reports. The sergeants were on his case, and he didn't want to lose his work assignment with his partner, Yackel Von Baerenzwinger, the department's canine.

*

With one eye on the police car and the other on the sheriff, Rosanna explained: "The heavy rain caused erosion of our garden's topsoil. I was just repairing the damage by collecting our soil."

"Yes, I see that," said Jennings, as he took additional photos with his cell phone. "I don't see anything wrong with you recovering your dirt. I'm just recording information for my report."

"I don't understand why you're making a report if there's nothing wrong," replied Rosanna.

Jennings smiled and nodded.

Rosanna waited. Despite this obese, uniformed deputy sheriff, wearing a holstered gun, and a military mustache, she wasn't frightened or intimidated by him, simply confused. His dog was another matter.

"Sometimes we gather information that we don't really think is necessary, but it's collected because it might be important later," he said.

Rosanna was listening. She was really trying to understand. "Did he just say that he was collecting information he didn't need?" She waited for a better explanation.

Jennings tried again to make sense out of something that (he admitted) didn't make sense. "As officers, we're given discretion to make decisions on our own. If I'd been driving by and observed you collecting dirt out of your ditch, I would have smiled and waved as I drove by. But when the public calls in to report a potential problem, something they believe is suspicious, we need to investigate in case of a follow-up call."

Rosanna still didn't comprehend. She quickly deduced, "This was English, not Amish thinking. I have no choice but to cooperate. Who would call the Sheriff's Office about me recovering God's topsoil? Who would think this is suspicious? And when would *Mam* and *Dat* return with our children?"

# 2

## Deputy Jennings and the Black Buggies

Driving his horse-and-buggy, Jacob Borntrager arrived at the scene of the so-called crime. He and his wife, Anna, carried a buggy-full of grandchildren—five of them belonging to Rosanna and Adam. Anna held the youngest in her arms. The other children remained curious but quiet as Jacob exited his trusted transportation.

Rosanna had been observing the buggy for several minutes as it neared the farmstead. She welcomed the clip-clop sound of the horse's hooves on the asphalt. She half-smiled at the neigh and whinny of the horse. Faith and family kept her strong. She exhaled a deep breath when she saw the faces of her parents and her children. Their worried eyes were big and unblinking, but their mouths relaxed the longer they stared at her standing safely beside the big, uniformed, English man.

Deputy Jennings had the information he needed for his case. He would be sure there wasn't a single blank box on the report form. Jennings was ready to go "10-8," to get back into service, to become available for the next assignment, but he knew that first he had more explaining to do.

Just then he heard a loud noise. It was his stomach growling. He was famished. Tom considered his next meal.

Jennings had watched the closed buggy pull into the driveway of the house, its rotating wooden wheels slowing to a stop. He was amazed that one horse could pull so many people. The buggy's engine was one horsepower, yet it carried two adults and how many children? From his patrol car he tried to count the number of straw hats and bonnets worn by the youngsters.

The Amish man, Jacob, and his daughter, Rosanna, were talking, but they were a fair distance away from the deputy. Jennings couldn't make out the words. He wondered if they were speaking Dutch or German.

Yackel started barking excitedly, which was extremely unusual unless he perceived a threat. Jennings visually scanned the area, but he didn't recognize any potential problems.

*"Nein!"* Jennings shouted, telling Yackel, "no," to stop barking. He considered letting Yackel out of the SUV for a bathroom break.

Jennings decided to wait until he was approached by the long-bearded Amish man wearing the common solid-colored shirt, dark blue pants held up with suspenders, and straw hat, before initiating a conversation. There wasn't much more for him to say that he hadn't already explained to Rosanna Yoder. He hoped they would understand. He was just doing his job.

But as he waited beside his patrol car, he spotted them. The distant black boxes, like hard-shelled turtles, approaching and growing larger. "Buggies!" he said out loud. "Lots of them!"

Rosanna and Jacob stopped talking and studied the road. Between the two of them, they gradually identified each advancing family by the subtle differences in their respective horses and Plain buggies.

Jennings thought back to the morning's patrol briefing. He didn't recall a request for traffic control at any funeral, but the horse-drawn buggies were approaching from both the north and the south. "What was going on?" he asked himself. He sure hoped that his location wasn't their intended destination.

Jennings' brain searched for an explanation. "Maybe the Amish buggies were headed to church for a wedding, a funeral, or a prayer meeting. Wait, did they even have churches? Should I call in deputies for traffic control? Was I the reason they were on the road?" Jennings imagined his radio call: "431, Dispatch, I've been surrounded by Amish buggies and need help! The Plain People are holding me down and shaving my mustache! Send all available Mennonites to render officer assistance."

Suddenly, Jennings became aware that his anxiety was spiking. He took deep breaths and considered his options. "I should notify my sergeant, just in case there's going to be an Old Order Amish uprising."

Tom had always heard that the Amish were not violent, that they were conscientious objectors when the country had a military draft. But still, couldn't they be armed with slingshots, pocketknives, heavy skillets, sharp kitchen knives, pitchforks, and hunting rifles? Or make explosives from natural fertilizer?

Jennings had a feeling that he was on the verge of learning a thing or two about cultural communication. He understood that the situation might become a personal test of his ability to help resolve conflict.

The first buggy, one of many, turned into the driveway. The Yoder house was their destination. Jennings tried to swallow. His only thought was a question: "What on earth have I got myself into?"

\*

"431 to 422," Deputy Jennings said into his police radio's microphone.

"Go ahead," replied Sergeant Hunter.

"Can you 10-23 with me at my assignment?"

"10-4, I'm nearby, but I'm encountering a lot of buggies and tractors moving in your direction."

"10-4, thanks," concluded Jennings, hoping the Amish church districts were gathering for a vote about the use of electricity, or meeting to discuss whether to permit their youth to play electronic games on their phones, if they owned any.

# 3

## Deputy Jennings Apologizes

Rosanna knew everyone, even the babies. She watched as the familiar buggies moved up the driveway and parked by the barn. Tractors stopped on the shoulder of the road as if they were prepared to participate in a farm auction. Like marching soldiers, teenage boys carried rakes and shovels over their shoulders. Women carted picnic boxes. Children of all sizes, momentarily at least, held each other's hands upon seeing the big English man with a holster and gun.

Jennings phoned Sgt. Hunter. He described the actions he had taken in preparation for his written report. He had only asked Mrs. Yoder the standard questions required—nothing else. Then, Jennings told Hunter that Rosanna's father, Jacob Borntrager, was nearby with his daughter.

Sgt. Hunter's voice was loud and excited. He repeatedly declared that he'd never heard of anything like this happening, if in fact the Amish were gathering due to one deputy asking a few standard questions. There had to be more to it. What had Jennings done?

"I'm calling our captain," said Hunter, "He likes to hear the bad news as soon as possible. Are you sure you didn't say or do anything offensive to her?"

"Nothing, except ask her age, date of birth, weight, color of hair, and phone number. I've heard that some Amish have phones. I can't believe that would cause an uprising. I mean, I didn't ask to see her driver's license or social security card. I didn't ask her out on a date! I'm sure she'd consider me a whale of a catch if she wasn't committed to her marriage and busy with cooking, canning, cleaning, sewing, and doing laundry."

"Have you ever considered that your odd sense of humor may have caused this trouble in the first place?" asked Hunter. "I'll be there in a minute. Don't do anything stupid."

Jennings' stomach growled. He found a candy bar, ripped the wrapper open, and shoved the sweet into his cavernous mouth. He wasn't happy. He felt like a scapegoat.

Yackel whimpered. He was hungry too, and he needed to pee. But he also wanted out of the car so he could meet the woman.

Meanwhile, the farm was getting as crowded as an Old Order Amish family reunion.

*

Hunter told Jennings that they'd find out soon enough what was going on, but the captain wanted this incident to end as soon as possible. If the Amish gathering was about Rosanna Yoder reclaiming her garden's dirt from the culvert, then the whole thing was a big, unfortunate misunderstanding. The 911 call would be no-cased, Jennings would apologize, and things would get back to normal.

\*

The two deputies approached Rosanna and her father, Jacob Borntrager. Anna had relocated to the barn with the grandchildren where she welcomed her neighbors.

"Mrs. Yoder," said Deputy Jennings, "this is Sgt. John Hunter, my supervisor."

"Hello," replied Rosanna. "This is my father, Jacob Borntrager. My husband is returning from Prairie Grove. He should be here shortly."

The uniformed deputies held out their hands and greeted Borntrager. Rosanna offered her hand, too, and the men shook it.

"After speaking with my sergeant," said Jennings, "I've learned that there's no need for me to make a report about the dirt being collected and returned to your garden. I made a mistake and I apologize."

Rosanna and Jacob hesitated before responding. They needed an extra moment for the words to make sense, to be sure they understood the correct meaning in English—their second language.

"So, you're saying we can help Rosanna and Adam with the job of repairing the erosion?" asked Jacob.

"Yes, that's correct," said Sgt. Hunter. "The Sheriff's Office wants you to know that we value you as good, responsible citizens. If we had more people like you, we'd have less work to do."

Without a word, Jacob gave a nearly imperceptible nod towards the house. Five teenage boys, relaxing on the front steps of the porch, stood in unison, grabbed their shovels and rakes, and headed to the ditch, ready to work.

"We do our best to mind our own business and not cause problems," said Jacob. "We also appreciate your concern when we're involved in car accidents and have large funerals. Those big trucks can create problems beyond blowing our hats off. One buggy accident is too many."

"Deputy Jennings, I have a question," stated Rosanna.

"Please, go ahead," said Jennings.

"All the information I gave you earlier, that you requested, will that remain in your computer?"

"Well . . ." Jennings hesitated.

"It will be deleted," said Hunter. "It's what we call a 'no-case.' There's nothing to investigate. It's over."

"Thank you," replied Rosanna.

"Yes, thank you," added Jacob, as he nodded.

The incident was over.

*

As Jennings handed out a personalized departmental business card to Mrs. Yoder and one to her father,

Mr. Borntrager, he said, "If I can ever be of help to you, here's my business card; just contact me," A moment later he realized his error. "I just gave my business phone number and email address to people without a phone or a computer! Well, they have my name in case they want to complain to the sheriff about my sense of humor or inappropriate cultural interaction."

Jacob invited both deputies to the barn to meet people and to sit down with them to share a community meal.

Jennings' stomach growled.

Yackel barked.

Rosanna touched her cheek.

Jennings excused himself, "I need to take care of Yackel," he said.

Two police radios squawked.

"422, 431, 10-48 at K96 and Orchard Rd. Ambulance responding."

"Sorry, we've got to go to a nearby injury accident," said Hunter, as he acknowledged the radio assignment with his walkie-talkie.

Rosanna was silent as her face turned a deathly ashen gray.

# 4

# Road and Bridge Department

Patrol Captain McArdle, on a smoke break outside the law enforcement center, received a return call from the Road and Bridge Department before his officers ever had an opportunity to return to the station to meet with him. The deputies were busy on an injury accident.

Kane, the assistant director of Road and Bridge, asked, "What's up?"

McArdle had a reputation for being direct, but since he had known Kane for twenty-five years, he asked a preliminary question.

"Kane," said McArdle, "How long have we known each other?"

Kane followed the script. "A long time, ever since the night we met on the ice-covered Arkansas River Bridge. You were working a fatality wreck and told me the county ought to have an electronic sign that warned people of icy bridges when conditions were severe. I told you that if people needed a warning sign about ice on a bridge in winter, then they shouldn't have a driver's license.

"Why do you ask how long we've known each other?" continued Kane. "Is your life of boozing finally catching up with you? Is your brain pickled?"

"I ask because you've always been concerned about your vehicles and heavy equipment being safe. You're quick to call me if they get vandalized or stolen. Now, for the first time, you're concerned about people stealing dirt. What's with that? Have your priorities changed? I must have missed the interdepartmental memo."

"I don't know what you're talking about," replied Kane. "Start at the beginning."

"One of my officers got dispatched to a theft-in-progress of county dirt from a county ditch. An Amish woman was retrieving her garden soil after last night's storm. The call came from your department."

"Oh . . . Who called it in?"

"I'm not even sure the caller gave his name. I hope it's your problem now. Because of the call, we were put in a tough situation. Even though we no-cased it, there may be repercussions. I'm still waiting to hear the details from my officers. I know the Amish have a reputation of forgiving others, but they have long memories, too. We overreacted."

"I'll do some checking. If it was one of my people, I'll find out what's going on. I'll deal with it. I've got a couple of workers who can get pushy, even aggressive, when it comes to farmers taking advantage of us by plowing and planting in our right-of-way. It causes us problems."

"Kane, we're not talking about a couple rows of field crop planted in a ditch; we're talking about soil eroding from a garden, an Amish garden."

"Okay, okay," said Kane. "I'm just trying to make sense of the call if it came from one of our employees."

"Thanks, Kane. I'm glad to hear you're on it. I knew you'd want to take care of it."

"I'll get to the bottom of this," promised Kane. "Thanks for the call."

# 5

## An Amish Accident

While Captain McArdle and Kane were on the phone, the asphalt on the county road near the Yoder farm, like a thermometer, was heating up after the night's sudden storm.

Rosanna, holding her youngest child, was standing beside her mother, Anna. They spotted Adam's tractor approaching from a half mile away. Rosanna waited by the mailbox and opened it twice before walking out into the county road so her view wouldn't be hampered by the parked tractors. Adam was alive!

Adam drove his tractor and horse trailer onto the property. When his feet hit the ground, Rosanna, still holding their baby, started talking in his ear. As they conversed about what the deputies had wanted, Anna held back.

They all migrated to the barn and joined their neighbors for a meal and conversation, but the peace didn't last long.

Within minutes, excited children trying not to hurry rushed in with news. A sheriff's car had returned, but it wasn't the big sheriff with the dog; it was an English woman in uniform with a gun and holster, who wore pants like a man, and had long hair past her shoulders!

The woman sheriff had asked the children to find Rosanna and Adam Yoder and have them meet her.

Rosanna and Adam quickly returned to their front driveway. "What now?" said Rosanna to Adam, "surely there hasn't been another accident."

"Hello," the deputy said. "I was sent here to locate the parents of two children who were in an accident with a truck. It appears they aren't hurt badly, but they did get thrown from their wagon."

"Do you know their names?" asked Adam.

"Yes," said the deputy as she glanced at her notebook. "Reuben and Rebecca Schrock, they're siblings."

"Twins. Yes, we know them; their parents are here," said Adam."

"You say, they are not hurt?" asked Rosanna, seeking confirmation.

"I haven't been at the scene of the accident, but I was told that an ambulance crew checked them out. The children said they just want to go home."

Adam left for the barn to find Milton and Irene Schrock, and one of their church district's ministers. Rosanna remained with the deputy.

"Can you tell me about the wreck?" asked Rosanna. "The deputies who were here earlier said it was an injury car accident."

"I haven't been to the wreck, but I know it was a hit-and-run. A silver Chevy truck drove straight into the horse. The horse died immediately, and the two teenagers were thrown off the wagon but not seriously hurt."

"Thank God for their lives being spared," said Rosanna.

"Yes, it sounds like the teens are scared but don't have any broken bones," the deputy said.

Rosanna introduced herself. "I'm Rosanna Yoder."

"Nice to meet you. I'm Christine Razer."

"Thank you for your help today, Christine. Here they come," said Rosanna, as she turned towards the Schrocks, Preacher Virgil Petersheim, and her husband, Adam.

After Deputy Razer assured the Schrocks that their children had survived the hit-and-run crash with no serious injuries, the parents accepted Razer's offer to be driven to the accident scene only four miles away, near the small country town of Humble.

However, with a degree of faith, Milton Schrock instructed their eighteen-year-old son, Marlin, to drive their tractor to the scene of the accident in case it was needed to haul away the wagon or dead horse.

Another tractor's engine started. The Schrock's would have neighborly assistance.

Adam and Rosanna said goodbye to Milton and Irene and promised to watch their other children.

Again, Adam and Rosanna walked back to their barn, remarking that their day was only half over, thankful the Schrock children were unhurt, saddened by the death of the horse.

# 6

# Deputy Jennings
# Works an Accident

Irene and Milton Schrock saw the emergency flashing lights ahead and glanced at one another. Deputy Razer slowed her patrol car.

Irene spotted the ambulance.

Milton observed his horse, dead, dismembered, lying on the road. The wagon, damaged, was on its side with one wheel visibly splintered into pieces.

"Where are our children?" Irene asked Deputy Razer.

"They're probably in the ambulance, waiting for us. Hold on a second," Razer replied, as she parked her car off the road.

Deputy Jennings approached Razer's patrol car and leaned over to speak to her through the open window.

"Thanks for helping us out," said Jennings.

"No problem," said Razer.

"We're the Schrocks," said Milton. "How are our children?"

"Your children will be glad to see you, thanks for coming. The paramedics and EMTs have examined them and would like to talk to you."

*

Like all deputies, Jennings' twelve-hour shift was a series of physical, mental, and emotional responses to 911 calls. One moment he was relaxed; a second later his body was jolted into emergency response mode. He enjoyed variety in his day, and the adrenaline rush was a welcome high, but it didn't help his blood pressure.

The trip from the Yoder's house to the injury accident site had taken less than five minutes, but during that time, Jennings, as always, had prepared for the worst and hoped for the best. When he and Hunter were told that they would arrive prior to the ambulance, it forced him to consider his limited life-saving skills. What would he need to do first if people were severely injured?

No one could miss the dead horse on the road or the overturned wagon. The scene was an awful sight with blood and innards smeared across the highway. It was as though the horse had been gutted by a powerful machine in a slaughterhouse. Jennings felt sorry for the horse, but he was still hopeful that the person who had reported the accident to 911 had been accurate about it involving only minor injuries to the passengers.

It took Jennings additional seconds to determine if the car parked on the shoulder of the road had been involved in the wreck. When he didn't observe any damage to it, he expected that it belonged to a Good Samaritan. While taking in the scene, his eyes searched for people, injured or dead.

He found two Amish teenagers sitting on the ground, on the other side of the parked car, speaking with a woman. The female adolescent, in a dark-green dress and bonnet, had a small cut to her forehead. The male, wearing a blue shirt and pants with suspenders, was holding his flattened straw hat.

Jennings was relieved to discover that no people were killed or seriously hurt. The youngsters had been "lucky" because they were alive, but they were unlucky to have been hit by a truck.

The emotional shift in Jennings was sudden. He was upbeat. Reuben and Rebecca Schrock, both seventeen, had scrapes and bruises, and they appeared stunned, but they were able to talk. They said they were sorry for the wreck that killed their horse and damaged their wagon.

Jennings and Hunter weren't paramedics or EMTs, but in short time their questions shifted from the well-being of the children to the investigation of the wreck. The person who had been involved in the accident with major damage, had left the scene. The driver had broken the law and needed to be caught before he hurt others, and to pay a penalty for his actions.

"Do you want a case on this?" Jennings asked Hunter, his face expressionless.

"Of course, I want a case on this!" Hunter responded. "It's a hit-and-run with major damage and injuries!"

"Okay, Sarge, just checking. I'm going to need to get personal information from the Amish teenagers. Is that 10-4?"

"Jennings, knock it off! It's a state requirement and you know it. We gotta do what we gotta do, Amish or not."

Jennings asked the teenagers what happened to cause the wreck.

"This truck came straight at us and hit our horse," answered Reuben. "There was no time for me to avoid it," he added.

"So, you were driving the wagon?" Jennings asked for verification.

"Yes, Rebecca and me, we were coming home from working at a neighbor's farm."

"Which way were you going and which way was the truck going?" Jennings inquired.

Reuben explained while Rebecca listened.

"Can you tell me what the truck looked like?" asked Jennings.

"It was a Chevrolet Silverado pickup truck. It was painted silver," he said, as his face instinctively lit up with excitement.

"Did you see a license plate?"

"No, I didn't think to look for a number. We were hit with the front of his truck, and it kept going in that direction," said Reuben, as he pointed towards the east.

"How about the driver? Was it a man or woman?"

"It was a man, English. He was the only person I saw in the truck."

"What race or color was he?"

"He was white, short hair, no beard, and no hat."

"How about his age?

"I don't know, in his twenties, probably."

"He looks like a man who works at a flower store in Prairie Grove," offered Rebecca. "He wasn't the man from the store, but he looks like him. I think he was at least twenty-one."

"I'm amazed that you're able to describe the driver," said Jennings, speaking to both Reuben and Rebecca. "If a truck was driving straight towards me, I would have been so scared, I'm not sure I'd be able to identify anyone, only the ditch."

"The man drove by once before he hit us," said Rebecca.

"Becca! *Nein!*"

Her response was immediate. She shut her mouth and looked at the ground.

Jennings studied them. "Have you seen the man before?" he asked. "Do you know him? Did he say anything to you?" For a second, Jennings wondered if the wreck could have been intentional, even a hate crime.

"That's the best we can do on a description of the man and the truck," said Reuben. "My back's starting to hurt now."

"I hear the ambulance," said Jennings. "Your lucky day. The medics will check you out."

"Can you go tell our parents to come get us?" asked Rebecca.

"Yes, we'll have someone do that. Let me confirm your address," he said.

Hunter took photos of the accident scene and collected evidence from the road. The wagon was torn up. Silver paint was embedded on the wooden wheel where it had been transferred from the hit-and-run truck. The sergeant also examined pieces of broken plastic from a headlight panel and shards from the truck's front window.

Blood was everywhere.

Flies swarmed the horse and its scattered remains.

# 7
## Deputy Jennings
## Learns a Lesson

It was God's will for the children to be in the wreck, but it was also His will for them to live. With the results of God's plans surrounding them, Milton and Irene Schrock were thankful. They also reminded themselves to limit their cooperation with law enforcement.

The parents appreciated the ride to the scene of the accident and for the medical services given to their children by the ambulance personnel.

Yes, the Schrock parents recognized that Reuben and Rebecca would be sore from their mishap. Aches and pains were to be expected. The adults would observe the youngsters for any unusual behavior, and if noted, would consider contacting medical experts.

When Deputy Jennings told the Schrocks that his agency had broadcast a radio alert telling officers to be on the lookout for the silver Chevrolet truck, the adults displayed a lack of interest in the procedure or the outcome. Instead of a concern for catching the suspect driver, the Schrocks explained that from their perspective the event was over.

Mr. Schrock wasn't keen on estimating the value of his horse and wagon. What was the purpose since they didn't believe in insurance, and they weren't interested in restitution?

Reluctantly, Schrock estimated the horse was worth at least $3,000, and the wheel, if it were the only part of the wagon requiring replacement, would cost about $200. But he was not interested in answering further financial questions.

Jennings prepared himself. If he paid attention, he was going to learn more about the Old Order Amish. He wanted to be respectful, yet he wanted to understand. None of his prior law enforcement training had covered Amish beliefs or customs.

The big deputy was no longer worried about getting into trouble with his agency. He wanted to do what he thought was the right thing. He would do his job *and* respect the Amish.

Standing beside the county road as the Schrock's dead horse and damaged wagon were hauled away wasn't the ideal place for a personal discussion about religion or culture. Jennings also understood that the children needed to get home and rest. They'd been through a lot. He was hot, tired, and dirty, and he hadn't been thrown into a ditch during a car wreck.

But he still wanted to learn all he could before he inadvertently fouled up another report involving the Amish. This time, if they would let him, he would do more than fill out computer boxes on a form. If possible, he wanted to connect with these people personally, not as a uniformed, uninformed, government official.

It wasn't Sunday school or a class on religious studies, but the Schrocks told the deputy as much as they felt they could without breaking their own Amish rules and community norms. The parents were generous with their time and knowledge although Milton did most of the talking.

God would decide the penalty for the driver of the truck, not them. They had no interest in assisting the government in arresting anyone for a worldly crime. In fact, their children would not, could not, testify in court if the English man were ever found.

Finally, Jennings learned, the Schrock family, including parents and children, had already forgiven the driver of the truck. It was done. They had prayed together and forgiven the reckless driver as soon as the paramedics released the children from the ambulance. Each Schrock had also personally thanked the lady who had stopped and helped the twins.

The Amish would repair their wagon and dispose of their horse. Life would continue. From the Amish point-of-view, no further action was necessary. Certainly, no publicity was desired.

Again, the Schrocks appreciated the deputies for their help. "Thank you very much," they repeated. But now, they needed to collect the rest of their family and go home. There were chores to do and a meal to prepare.

No, a business card was not wanted, they answered when Jennings offered. Accepting it would be a sign of cooperation with the government.

They didn't want a reminder about the day. Instead, they just wanted to get back to their routine life of separatism. It was God's will.

# 8

# Blame the Amish

Arthur Kane was Assistant Director of the Cottonwood County Road and Bridge Department. He'd been around longer than the furniture and felt as worn out as the old carpet.

Kane was following up on a call he had received from the Sheriff's Office. One of Kane's people had contacted Emergency Dispatch and reported a theft in progress. The property allegedly being stolen was soil from a county ditch.

According to Patrol Captain McArdle, an employee of the Road and Bridge Department had created a headache for law enforcement by initiating the inaccurate, if not prejudicial, phone call. McArdle, known as "Mac," didn't want any more unnecessary calls. Understandably, no one, especially an innocent person, liked being investigated for criminal behavior.

As Mac explained to Kane, his officers hadn't really accused anyone of anything, but they were gathering personal information, doing their job. Since the woman interviewed was just collecting her runaway garden soil, the whole response was one big fat farce, and it made the Sheriff's Office look bad. Mac wanted to avoid any repeat occurrences.

Kane agreed with Mac. The odd call created needless drama.

Now Kane was prepared to have a one-on-one conversation with Harley Beasley, the employee in question.

\*

"But it's county soil!" explained Beasley. "State statute gives us the right to control that soil. What if everyone dug their own ditches? Put in their own culverts? You know what would happen. It would be chaotic! Our mission is to protect the roads by maintaining proper and effective drainage."

Kane let him talk.

"The farmers already do their own thing. They ignore us. They tear down their fences so their gigantic equipment can plow, and plant, and harvest in *our* right of way! They fill up *our* ditches and make extra work for us. They don't care. If they want to donate their soil to us, then it's ours for the taking."

Beasley wasn't done.

"If I was farming, I'd stop tearing up the perimeter grasses. In my landscaping business, I help my customers conserve their soil and water."

Kane waited.

"And the Amish tear up our roads with their horses and tractors, and they don't pay taxes, and it's unsafe the way they carry their families to town in the back of trailers. They wouldn't recognize a seat belt if they sat on one!"

Beasley finally stopped.

"So," said Kane, "it's accurate to say that you called Dispatch to report the Amish woman stealing soil from our county ditch?"

"That's right, and I'd do it again," replied Beasley. "I hope the Sheriff's Office puts a stop to the theft. I hope they threatened her with jail time. Boss, we need to be proactive. Things are going to hell."

Kane didn't expect that Beasley would change his perspective, but he was going to explain things, then give his subordinate a direct order. Any further concerns that Beasley had while on duty regarding county soil in county ditches would start and stop with Kane. Simply put, if Beasley contacted Emergency Dispatch or the Sheriff's Office about dirt being stolen in any ditch, Beasley would be fired.

"Okay," Kane said, "Listen up, we don't arrest people for planting crops in our ditches. We don't arrest people for retrieving their garden soil after flooding. We have our procedures. We work with the County Counselor, and she sends out certified letters, and we schedule meetings with the offenders, and sometimes we even send out bills when landowners have created problems for us that we've had to correct. But these are procedures we manage *without* calling law enforcement. Understand?"

"I understand, but I don't agree with this weak approach; we can do better," responded Beasley.

"Follow county procedures and you'll stay out of trouble," said Kane.

"Let me respond to some of your complaints," Kane continued. "I shouldn't need to do this, but you're a valuable employee; I want to give you a chance to look at this differently. You've probably heard this all before, but here's my view on how we do our job."

Now it was Beasley who was quiet.

"Sure, farmers could make our job a lot easier," said Kane. "Sometimes I don't know if they don't know better or they just don't care. I've seen them plant in our right-of-way and then be unable to harvest the crop due to the abrupt drop off. I've heard their complaints when we spray and kill their runaway crops. And, over the years, I know we've hauled away tons and tons of their blowing topsoil. That's just the way it is. I keep reminding myself that most people aren't criminals; they're just doing the best they can do."

"But we have state statutes on our side," countered Beasley.

"And the Amish, by far, aren't the problem. They don't tear down their fences or ignore erosion. They rotate their crops. They, better than most, manage the soil. It's in their blood. It's who they are. And they understand that bigger isn't necessarily better.

"I've heard you complain before about the Amish not paying taxes, and others have corrected you, so I have to wonder why you continue degrading them."

"They don't license their tractors or buggies," said Beasley, "so they're using our roads for free."

"The Amish don't use the roads very much compared to the rest of us; it's not like they're taking a cross-country trip to Florida for the winter on a tractor. At least around here they have air in their tires, but true, they don't pay an annual user fee for their tractors to operate on the highway for when they go shopping or to market their products. If you think about it, the horse-and-buggy Amish don't do much damage to our roads, and they sure don't contribute to air pollution like our motor vehicles."

"What does air pollution have to do with roads?" asked Beasley.

"Hold on, I'm trying to give you a big picture to counter your biased attitude.

"As I was saying, Amish pay local, state, and federal taxes. They pay income taxes, real estate taxes, property taxes, sales taxes, inheritance taxes, and capital gains taxes. I know they don't pay Social Security, but they don't use it. They pay taxes for public schools but may never send their children to one. Instead, they usually pay their own private elementary school teachers to instruct their children on the basics. You could say the Amish pay twice as much as others for their children's elementary education."

"That's their choice," said Beasley, not persuaded. "They could send their children to public school."

"Speaking of choice," said Kane, "the Amish have made a choice to be separate from us when it comes to their religion and culture. It's called freedom of religion."

"I'm in favor of freedom of religion. Who could be against that?" asked Beasley.

"I figured you'd be for it because I know you're active with your church."

"But we pay our taxes."

"You do? If you investigate it, you'll see your church doesn't pay income tax because it's a nonprofit. It's exempt from federal, state, and local taxes."

"So, we should just let everyone tear up our roads and ditches?" challenged Beasley.

"You're not listening. I didn't say that, and you know it's not what I think. We have limits on what we can do. We do our best. That's what I expect out of you. Starting today, right now, I expect you to contact me whenever you have an urge to call law enforcement and complain about people tearing up our ditches or roads.

"There's no wiggle room on this, Harley. This is how we operate. We have our procedures, and you need to follow them like everyone else. I won't give you preferential treatment when I hold everyone else accountable for their actions. Do you understand?"

"Yeah, I understand," said Beasley, looking down at his hands, no longer challenging his boss.

"Good, I'll get a letter of understanding for you to sign so we won't be having this same conversation down the road."

Beasley's eyes shot up and stared at Kane. "I don't need another letter in my file, I understand," said Beasley.

"Harley, remember what I just said about procedure. This is the county procedure. Now get back to work and make me proud. Just leave the farmers and the Amish to me. That's not your job. It's mine.

"Go on, get out of here."

# 9

## Tom and Jesse Jennings
## Discuss Parenting

At home, Tom shared his day with his wife, Jesse.

Their children, Julia, and Hannah, were in their rooms for the night. Tom and Jesse watched the TV news. Tom attacked a bag of potato chips and dip. Jesse ate grapes. Occasionally, their phones would buzz, and they would glance at messages.

"Today, for the first time, I had an opportunity to interact with an Amish family, beyond talking about the weather," said Tom to Jesse. "I learned something about their beliefs, and I'd like to visit them again."

"That's nice," stated Jesse. "You've told me before about conversations with Amish men. I know you like those cute, young, Amish waitresses at Amanda's Amish Kitchen. What was different about today?" she asked.

"At the end of one crazy assignment, I got invited to a community meal. It never actually happened because we had to go to an accident, but the invitation made me feel appreciated. Then, at the scene of the wreck, I learned why Amish don't get involved in reporting crime."

"I've read about that," said Jesse. "It's because they want to remain separate from the outside world."

"That's right, and it's because they believe in forgiveness. They don't want to prosecute a person. Instead, they leave it up to God."

"So, they won't help law enforcement solve a crime?" asked Jesse.

"I don't know if they would help us catch a murderer or not. I would hope so. But today I learned from one family that they wouldn't help us prosecute the hit-and-run driver who nearly killed their children when he ran into their horse-and-wagon. They don't want restitution either."

"That's hard to believe," said Jesse. "If someone hurt one of our girls, I'd want the person locked up for life. Just throw away the key."

"Yeah, it sure makes me aware how differently we think about punishment," said Tom. "My job is to catch 'em. Their job is to forgive 'em."

"I wonder if they punish their children or not," said Jesse. "They must do a pretty good job of parenting; I haven't seen any Amish on the FBI's ten most wanted list."

Tom laughed. "Neither have I. We can learn something from them. We've sure had problems lately with Hannah and Julia."

"I don't know if the girls fight more often than other children," said Jesse, "but the part that's disturbing to me is how long they can hold a grudge."

"Yeah, they're reluctant to forgive one another," said Tom.

"And I don't know why," said Jesse. "We've raised them well."

"We love them dearly; we'd do anything for them," said Tom, "but it would be great to solve this riddle about holding grudges."

"I can google that again on my phone," said Jesse, "but everyone has a different opinion. You and I forgive one another, but we rarely argue. Maybe we need to fight more often and show the girls how we patch things up!" said Jesse as she laughed.

Tom crunched his last potato chip, then used his index finger to take one last swipe at the empty container of cream cheese with chili sauce dip. "We could take away their phones," he said, seeking an easy answer, but one that hadn't worked before.

"Your Amish friends must have a solution. I've heard they have church seven days a week. We could try that."

"When would we work?" asked Tom, knowing Jesse wasn't serious.

She continued. "They can't take away phones from their children since they aren't allowed to have them."

"I'm not sure whether phones are still forbidden," said Tom. "When we worked that accident near Humble, in no time at all, Amish arrived to assist."

"Well," continued Jesse, "I don't think they tell their teenage children, 'Until you forgive your sister, you're grounded. We're taking away your horse-and-buggy privileges.'"

Tom chuckled. "The Old Order Amish know something we don't. Maybe it has to do with priorities. You know how Julia gets when we tell her to turn off her phone at night."

"Yeah," agreed Jesse, "she told me last night she needs it for an alarm clock! When was the last time she got out of bed without me waking her up? She gets nervous with it on, and she gets anxious with it off. Take your pick."

"Since she turned ten," said Tom, "I don't think her head's ever been clear from screen time. It could be a cause of trouble; I don't know. It's a different world than the one we grew up in. We didn't have a smart phone within reach twenty-four hours a day."

"I have an idea," said Tom. "We need to send our girls to Amish Camp! No phones. No TV. Instead, Julia and Hanna could learn how to contribute to a working family farm, weed the garden, clean out horse stalls, and churn butter."

"I know you're joking," said Jesse, "but it would be an opportunity for the girls. Maybe we can create something like that here at home without giving up electricity."

"Agreed, let's figure something out," said Tom as he felt his phone vibrate. "We can learn about cutting back from so many electronics. I might be able to get ideas from the Amish."

"Good luck with that," said Jesse. "I've heard they're not too anxious to share their customs. What would you say? 'Our life is bombarded with agitating media messages; can you help?'"

"I don't think it can hurt to try," Tom answered. "The Schrocks are dairy farmers who sell extra milk and butter on the side. I'll stop by and ask for ideas. We're low on butter."

"Okay, Tom," agreed Jesse, "but remember the sergeants have been after you to focus on doing your job. You said Hunter was upset with you about the assignment involving erosion of the garden soil."

"Yeah, but after today I'm thinking I can do my job without worrying so much about my supervisors. Hunter had a closer look at how one crackpot citizen complaint can create a bizarre situation for the department, especially when we're dealing with a closed community. I think the Amish can teach us something, and I think I can support them. If they prefer not to explain a custom or belief to me, I can accept that."

"Okay, honey, but don't go Amish on me. I wouldn't mind learning how to sew a quilt, but we agreed that two children were all we wanted," said Jesse as she held back a smile.

"Yes, I remember," said Tom, straight-faced, "although there's a saying that things are cheaper by the dozen. And, we can always add on bedrooms to the house."

Jesse held her silence and waited for him to assure her he was joking about any more children.

As Tom licked the grease and salt from the potato chip bag—which he had turned inside-out—he finally responded, "Agreed, lately, we've had our hands full enough with only two kids."

# 10
## Deputy Jennings
## Interviews a Suspect

The unfortunate accident was his good fortune.

Thanks to the Schrocks, Tom Jennings felt like he, for the first time, had a better understanding of the Amish. He was pleased they shared what they did. It would have been easier for them to say nothing to an outsider. Generally, remaining silent about their beliefs was the Amish community's way.

After the wreck, Jennings decided to do his job despite knowing that the Schrocks were not interested in pursuing an investigation. As per departmental policy, he prepared a brief media report of the accident. It included a description of the hit-and-run vehicle. However, Jennings purposely excluded the names of the Schrock children.

*

Ironically, a crime involving Plain People was solved due to modern technology. The Public Information Officer posted the hit-and-run information about the Amish horse-and-wagon accident on social media. Then, an anonymous caller responded to the post and gave the location of a truck that fit the description of the suspect vehicle.

\*

The day after the wreck, once Jennings was notified of the helpful call, he easily located the suspect vehicle parked in a driveway at a residential address in Prairie Grove. With the front window shattered, the truck had obviously been in a head-on collision.

\*

Deputy Jennings had considered what approach to take if he ever got an opportunity to interview the owner of the vehicle. The officer prepared himself to hear half-truths and blatant lies.

- "I don't know anything about any accident."

- "I don't remember anything. I must have hit my head."

- "Someone stole my truck and returned it."

- "I always leave my truck unlocked with the keys in the ignition."

- "I better not say anything until I speak to an attorney."

\*

Before the man who answered the door could identify himself, Jennings observed the cuts on the man's face and swelling around his left eye. Excitedly, he knew, "this is the guy!"

After introductions, Jennings pointed to the Chevy truck and asked Shawn Harris, "Is that your vehicle?"

"Yeah, it sure is."

"I'm here because I'm investigating a hit-and-run accident that occurred yesterday."

"That's the truck," offered Harris.

"I'm also looking for the driver," Jennings continued.

"That's me," responded Harris.

Jennings was thrown off from his standard questioning. He hadn't expected this. It was too easy. "Something's wrong," thought Jennings. "This isn't normal. Criminals evade questioning. Isn't Harris a criminal?"

Harris agreed to allow Jennings to examine the truck more closely. Photos were taken, horsehair and paint chips were recovered as evidence, driver's license and insurance information recorded. Everything went so smoothly that Jennings considered it unnecessary to have the truck towed for evidence. It would have been a wasteful expense.

Not reporting an injury accident was a serious traffic offense, so Jennings continued to be surprised by Harris' cooperation.

"This guy is facing jail time," thought Jennings. "What's the rest of his story?"

Harris recounted to Jennings that he'd been at a party in the country and had, he knew, too much beer to drink. Usually, his girlfriend was his designated driver, but she couldn't attend the party, so he had stayed overnight to give himself a chance to sober up. The problem was, in the morning he'd started drinking again and then drove himself home. He decided to take back roads to avoid the sheriff, but then he realized he was lost. He turned his truck around to ask nearby Amish for help, to find out the nearest road to town. Shortly after he turned around, the accident happened.

He remembered a runaway horse-and-buggy. "The horse unexpectedly swerved towards my truck," explained Harris. "There wasn't time for me to stop. I got scared, and since I'd been drinking, I didn't report the accident until today.

"I'm sorry I left the scene of the accident. Was the Amish couple hurt?"

"*You* reported it today?" asked Jennings, dumbfounded.

"Yes, when I saw the Facebook post with the description of my truck, I knew I had to do the right thing. I called the number listed and they thanked me for getting involved with fighting crime."

Jennings was pleased with himself for having the suspect vehicle's description posted and he was thrilled that Harris had owned up to his actions.

"Are the people, okay?" Harris asked again. "I owe them an apology."

"They're recovering from their scrapes and bruises. You know you killed their horse; he's dead."

"Oh, the horse! I'll never forget the terror in his eyes. I'm *so* sorry."

# 11

## Deputy Jennings
## Stops a Speeder

Two weeks after the horse-and-buggy accident, Deputy Jennings was on duty working traffic with his trusted companion, K-9 Yackel Von Baerenzwinger.

It was Saturday night and Jennings was out "hunting." He knew there were drunk drivers and druggies to catch, who needed to go to jail. "Maybe, for a few hours at least, I can help make the road a little safer for everyone, including the drunks," he thought.

As a vehicle approached him with its high beams blazing, he flicked his patrol car's high beams on and off, but the approaching driver ignored the visual cue. Jennings slowed, in preparation to turn around and follow the truck. "Was the driver busy on his phone or intoxicated?" he wondered. Drunk and drugged drivers were incapable of concentrating on too many things at once. Safe driving required people to use all their faculties.

Jennings quickly caught up to the truck and observed its movements. It didn't take long before the driver couldn't maintain control of the vehicle. The tires drifted outside the designated lane. When the next car approached, again, the suspect driver didn't lower his vehicle's high beams.

As Jennings kept pace with the truck, he checked his speed and determined the driver was traveling about ten miles over the posted limit. In preparation to stop the truck, the deputy drew closer. He had witnessed enough for a valid traffic stop: driver not lowering high beams when approaching other vehicles, tires left of center, and speeding.

The patrol car's headlights revealed a silver Chevrolet truck with two-by-fours extending past the open tailgate, and a Kansas license plate displaying a current Cottonwood County sticker. Two back-seat passengers appeared to be adult white females.

Prior to stopping the truck, Jennings ran the license tag through dispatch.

"Dispatch to 431."

"Go ahead, Dispatch."

"Kansas, 408, F-Frank, K-King, W-William, returns on a 2015 Chevrolet truck to Shawn Harris, 125 Skyview, Prairie Grove, Kansas."

"10-4, thanks," acknowledged Jennings. "Also, request a 10-27 on the registered owner. He may be suspended."

"10-4," the dispatcher responded. Almost immediately, she added, "10-4, confirming the 10-27 shows DL suspended on Shawn L. Harris . . ."

"10-4, 10-6 traffic with this vehicle at Sandbur Road on K61."

"10-4, 431, 10-6 traffic on K61 at Sandbur Road, possible suspended driver."

Suddenly, after activating the patrol car's emergency lights and siren, the dark night lit up like a Christmas concert with multiple strobe lights. The suspect vehicle suddenly jerked to the side of the road. Jennings left his high beams on to make it more difficult for the driver to monitor his approach.

Yackel was excited, anxious, saliva drooling from his mouth like Pavlov's laboratory dog. He recognized this familiar activity as an opportunity for him to get outside, find his ball, and to play.

"*Sitz*! (sit) *Bleib*! (stay)," Jennings barked at Yackel.

It took Jennings too long to exit his patrol vehicle. In a real emergency he wouldn't have been safe. He'd have been a big stationary target. His rolls of fat caught on the steering wheel and his walkie-talkie, attached to his belt, got tangled in the seat belt. Finally, his feet hit the ground.

Huffing and puffing, Jennings approached the stopped truck and prepared himself, unconsciously touching his handcuff case and holster. He knew one thing for sure, "Shawn Harris was going to jail."

Jennings, as usual, was alert to the potential risks of his surroundings, especially the interior of the targeted vehicle. There were four people to watch: two women in the back seat and two white males in the front. With his flashlight, Jennings did a cursory check of the backseat and front, checking for weapons and open containers of alcohol.

As the deputy stopped outside the driver's window, he heard a welcoming, upbeat greeting from the front-seat passenger: "Hello, Officer Jennings! Good to see you again!"

Jennings did a double take. Shawn Harris was in the front passenger seat, *not* behind the wheel.

The deputy looked at the driver who appeared frozen, staring out the front window, both hands tightly gripping the steering wheel in the ten and two o'clock position.

"You know Reuben," Harris continued, "although you might not recognize him driving my truck."

The driver still didn't move.

Jennings tried to think of anyone he knew by the name of Reuben.

"Reuben Schrock?" asked Jennings.

The driver slowly turned his head to face Jennings. "I have a driver's license," he said, "I got it today at the Department of Motor Vehicles. It's printed on paper. They said they were going to send me a laminated one in the mail."

"Great! I'll have a look at it in a minute," said Jennings, as he observed the driver's eyes—they were clear, not bloodshot—and checked Reuben's breath for alcohol by deeply inhaling the air, imitating drug-sniffing Yackel, but he was unable to detect any scent of the intoxicant.

"He's a pretty good driver, don't you think?" asked Harris.

Jennings ignored Harris. "Reuben, on the driver's test do you remember anything about headlights having both low and high beams?"

"Yes, Shawn told me."

"Well, that's why I stopped you. When you don't lower your headlight beams, it's harder for others to drive safely. You about blinded me."

"Told you, Reuben," said Harris.

"Sorry," added Reuben.

Jennings tried to accept what he was seeing. Reuben Schrock, the Amish wagon driver, who was a hit-and-run victim of Shawn Harris, was wearing store-bought clothes, and he was driving the same truck that had damaged the Schrock wagon and killed their horse.

It was too much for Jennings. Without moving his feet, he inspected the front window. Even with the splattered insect carcasses, he could tell it had been recently installed. He touched the outside edge of the window with his left hand and pressed a finger into the soft putty.

It was mind-boggling. Jennings knew he was on a traffic stop, not attending a social gathering, but he wanted more information. He had so many questions about Reuben and Harris being together. "How had it happened?"

"431 to Dispatch," said Jennings, "information only, everything's 10-4, I'll be 10-6 here for a while. That 10-27 you ran, he's not driving."

"10-4, 431," dispatch replied. "Information only, any unit responding to 431's location can 10-22. No need for acknowledgement."

The women in the back seat had been quiet, but attentive to the conversations. "Are either of you Rebecca Schrock?" asked the deputy.

Both women laughed and said "no." Rebecca was Reuben's twin sister.

"This is Dot, my girlfriend," said Harris, as he turned sideways and smiled at her sitting behind the driver's seat. "That's Katie, Reuben's Amish girlfriend," he continued as he pointed a thumb behind his seat. "They buy their English clothes at Walmart."

Reuben started shifting in his seat, uncomfortable. "She's not my girlfriend; we're going group bowling," he said.

"*Bowling?*" asked Jennings, as his head recoiled.

The car erupted into laughter as they all proclaimed, "It's true! We are! We're on our way to the bowling alley right now."

Harris said, "If you don't believe us, look in the back. You'll see that me and Dot have our bowling ball bags back there. We're in a bowling league."

Jennings needed reassurance that he was indeed conscious, lucid, and not hallucinating. He stepped away for a moment and used his flashlight to spot the two bowling ball bags beside the lumber in the bed of the pickup.

Serious as a heart attack, Jennings asked Reuben, "Have you run away?"

"No, I still live at home with my parents," said Reuben, "but this is *rumspringa* for Katie and me. It's an Amish word that means running-around days."

Katie spoke up, joining the conversation. "It's a period when young people like us, sixteen or older, consider their future. It's like your college years, only we don't pay tuition and we don't have homework."

"Okay then," said Jennings.

"Reuben, let me see your driver's license. If it's a valid DL, I'll let you go without a ticket, but slow it down. You were speeding."

"Told you," Harris said again.

Jennings secured Reuben's temporary driver's license, examined it, and prepared to check its validity using his patrol car's laptop. Instead, he handed it back to the driver.

"Use your low beams and slow down," said Jennings.

Shaking his head, Jennings glanced at each person in the truck, and said a group goodbye, "I'll let you get on your way. Have fun bowling."

# 12
## Bowling Alley Talk
## about Jersey Schrock

"Kate, if you need any help finding the right ball, let me know, okay?" asked Dot.

"Thanks, I'm looking for the same one I used before," answered Katie.

"Dot!" someone yelled from a distance.

Dot turned around and saw Coach Carter approaching with her arms spread wide open.

"Coach, it's great seeing you again!" said Dot as the two hugged. "I didn't know you ever got over here. Are you scouting?"

"No, just meeting friends; they should be here any minute," explained Coach.

Katie returned, holding a bowling ball. She waited.

Dot turned to Katie and said, "Kate, this is a friend of mine, we call her Coach; if you ever want tips on your bowling, she's the one to ask, only she's usually in Wichita."

"Nice to meet you," said Katie.

"Any friend of Dot's is a friend of mine," said Coach, as she held out her hand and the two greeted each other.

Katie smiled, but she wasn't sure what else to do. Coach was English, as old as her grandmother, her hair shorter than Reuben's, and her skin as dark as the short-sleeved shirt the woman wore. It had her name "Coach" stitched into the shiny fabric and the words "Go Shockers!" on a sleeve. Unlike Katie, Coach wore long pants.

Katie's blouse and skirt, along with her free-flowing straight hair, were monumental changes for her. In the Amish world, an hour earlier, she had worn a typical, long, plain-colored dress with her hair hidden, not on public display.

Starting with the name Dot, Katie added this lady's name to her list of other English people she had met recently.

Katie imagined the conversation she'd have with her mother the next day when she was grilled about what she had done tonight. "Oh, nothing," Katie would reply, "just hung out and talked with my new friends, Dot and Coach."

Her mother would know immediately they were English, but she would still need to ask, "Are they girls or boys?"

"We're taking our new friends bowling tonight," said Dot to Coach.

"Oh, I see Shawn's already got a lane," said Coach, looking towards the bowling lanes.

"Let's go say hello," said Dot. "I'll introduce you to Reuben, Kate's boyfriend."

The women joined the men by the lanes. Introductions followed.

Now it was Shawn's turn to compliment Coach. "I raised my average ten points by following Coach's advice. Thanks again, Coach."

"My pleasure, Shawn. Anytime."

"One of these days Reuben and Kate might want some tips from you," said Shawn, "but for now they're stuck with us."

"Do you two attend Prairie Grove High School?" asked Coach.

"No, we're out of school," replied Reuben.

"They're Amish, they live near Humble," added Shawn, "and they don't believe in high school so they're not on a bowling team . . . yet."

Reuben liked Shawn but he was getting a little tired of his new friend being an expert on the Amish. Even though Reuben had just met Coach, he wanted to correct the narrative.

"We believe in learning what we need to know for our work and family," said Reuben, "but we're not supposed to be exposed to too many changes outside the Amish.

"What am I saying?" thought Reuben. "I'm defending the Amish way while I'm dressed in English clothes and getting ready to bowl!

"Some students or scholars work and study through a vocational program called 'On the Farm' after they turn fourteen," Reuben continued. "I studied through my parents and a teacher."

"Our parents don't want us to grow up away from the farm or the religion," added Katie. "Did you know that the United States Supreme Court decided in 1972 that we couldn't be forced to attend school past the eighth grade?"

"Yes," answered Coach. "*Wisconsin vs. Yoder*. It decided the law was unconstitutional because it violated the Amish rights under the First Amendment which guarantees free exercise of religion."

Katie was always surprised when people outside the Amish knew about the legal case.

"What are your last names?" Coach asked.

"I'm a Schrock," said Reuben.

"I'm a Knepp," answered Katie.

Looking at Reuben, Coach asked, "Do you have any relatives with the first name of Jersey?"

Reuben thought for a second. It was an unusual person's name. "I don't know of anyone by that name, but we raise Jersey dairy cows," replied Reuben.

"When I attended Wichita State back in the 1980's, there was an incredibly talented football player named Jersey Schrock," said Coach. "He was from Cottonwood County and lived near Humble."

Reuben didn't know what else to say. He didn't know a Jersey Schrock. He'd already told her that.

"He only played two years because the college disbanded the football team after the 1986 season," Coach continued. "I never heard what happened to Jersey. If he would have gone professional, I know the media would have jumped all over that story. As a college sophomore he was already a standout player. He played the offensive line and had a stellar reputation for protecting the quarterback."

"I never heard of him either," said Shawn. "Of course, that was way before our time."

Shawn caught himself, "Well, not that long ago," said Shawn, a little embarrassed as he considered Coach's age.

"I'm no spring chicken," commented Coach. "It was thirty-five years ago, but about ten years back the WSU Alumni Association held a special celebration at Cessna Stadium for former football players and coaches. I was there in the audience, looking for Jersey, but he never showed up."

"Maybe he's dead," said Shawn.

"Yes, he could be dead," agreed Coach. "It's been a long time since my college days, but I remember one thing for sure about Jersey Schrock. He was raised Amish."

# 13
## Milton's Memories

The late morning heat guaranteed the afternoon would be a scorcher. Milton Schrock, in his horse-and-buggy, headed towards Amanda's Amish Restaurant to meet his old friend, Brian McDonald.

He reflected on their friendship.

It was a year since Milton had seen Brian. It was over thirty years since they had played college football and roomed together at Wichita State University.

What an amazing journey Milton had taken from Humble to Wichita and back. From the simple life to the modern world. From hand milking dairy cows to protecting Brian in ferocious football games. From traveling in a slow-moving horse-and-buggy in sub-zero weather to experiencing ear-popping, barf-bag airplane rides while traveling to distant intercollegiate competitions.

And off the field, Brian had protected Milton. Choosing a future life was difficult for all teenagers. For Milton, it was much harder. In their own way, Amish and English life were both appealing. Because of Brian, Milton had experienced the English world long enough to determine that he wasn't meant for it, or it wasn't meant for him.

Despite years of English exposure, Milton rarely thought of his adventurous youth until Brian's postcard arrived as a precursor to sitting down to relive the good old days. As a parent, Milton had learned what every other parent eventually accepted: Children were a test, especially if they acted the way their parents did when they were teenagers.

Irene, Milton's wife, had reminded Milton on numerous occasions that as much as they wanted their children to join the church, sometimes God worked in mysterious ways, on his own timetable. Milton was proof of that.

For a few years as a teenager and young adult, Milton had even owned a car. When home, he parked it behind the dairy barn. Everyone in the Amish community knew of his extended *rumspringa*. Neighbors were judgmental about his worldly choices. The parents who criticized the loudest would be fortunate if someday they didn't find themselves in a similar dilemma with their own children or grandchildren exploring English temptations, including drugs, sex, and violence. In fact, Milton could think of two friends who had never joined the Old Order Amish Church. One had joined the Beachy-Amish and the other found a Mennonite congregation to his liking.

After the university's football program disbanded in 1986, Milton's sophomore year, he decided that the world outside of the Amish was too fast paced, too foreign, and too isolating. For a few years he'd been fascinated with all the worldly possibilities. Why drive a horse-and-buggy when there were cars? Why work night and day, and go to church when one could party? Why stand out as Amish when English clothes could reduce the feeling of being constantly stared at and judged?

Ultimately, Milton's friends and family, especially Irene, had been a stronger influence than football, the English, and worldly conveniences. Deciding to be Amish meant choosing its traditions, rules—including following the *Ordnung*, a code of conduct that the church maintained—and religion. At times he found the rules difficult to accept. Had he been a church member and decided to further his education past the eighth grade, especially attend college, he would have been excommunicated by his bishop. But, since his participation in two years of college preceded his formal church membership, he wasn't punished at all.

Eventually, Milton's fears and his faith caught up with him. Every time his football team traveled by air, during every landing, he imagined a fiery crash and the horrors of hell if he died outside the Amish church. And during safe times, when he was home with his parents, siblings, and extended family, his community constantly prayed for him and pressured him. No English outsider could ever fathom the level of stress a young adult felt while deciding whether to leave or stay.

Irene was pivotal in his decision to join. Although she attended some WSU home football games at Cessna Stadium, and watched him protect his English friend, Brian, she had no desire to ever leave her Amish way of life—and Milton never expected she would.

After the biggest decision of Milton's life—joining church—he conscientiously participated in baptismal classes taught by his ministers and bishop. Upon completion of the instruction, during a church service held in his parents' own house, Milton proclaimed his willingness to serve God in faith and obedience. He was warmly welcomed as a new member of the Old Order Amish. Within three months he and Irene were married.

As Milton, in his buggy, passed by Humble's public elementary school, he recalled meeting Brian. Milton viewed the baseball field, thought he heard echoes of cheering, and remembered his participation in a three-legged race with Brian during the town's Frontier Days. Their friendship began at the summer celebration when they took a liking to one another, each respectful and curious of the other's culture.

It was a day of firsts for Milton. Up until then he had never known an African American.

As Milton's horse automatically halted at the familiar two-way stop sign, he swished his tail at bloodthirsty flies. Milton prepared himself for the visit. Approaching Amanda's Amish Kitchen parking lot, Milton tried to recall what sort of vehicle Brian had been driving on his last visit.

After parking his buggy in the shade under trees, he walked through the restaurant's parking lot already smelling the aroma of freshly baked bread. Milton nodded his head when he saw a State of Illinois license plate and recognized a familiar college icon—a window decal of a Wichita State University Shocker.

# 14

# Old Friends at
# Amanda's Amish Kitchen

Brian McDonald mailed his annual postcard to Milton Schrock. The color photo showed a Pennsylvania Amish farm with rows of grain stalks standing up in orderly fashion.

Two Saturday's later, Brian, as was tradition, sat at a table in Humble's only restaurant, Amanda's Amish Kitchen. He stared out a window that faced the public elementary school's playground where he viewed the baseball field.

Memories flooded Brian's head.

It was 1983 and Brian was seventeen, a senior at Prairie Grove High School. He was the starting quarterback for the school's football team. As part of the team's early summer conditioning program, the players participated in various tournaments that were not directly related to the gridiron.

A tug-of-war contest was the event that had brought Brian and his athletic peers to Humble, a small town just ten miles southeast of Prairie Grove. Because of the town's annual Frontier Days, Brian first met Milton.

Brian's tug-of-war team, the Bulldogs, defeated a local Amish group of boys thrown together at the last minute. "The Steelies," who had haircuts resembling the Beatles from the early 1960s, had muscle but no experience or strategy. No wonder the locals lost. However, one boy, due to his size and strength, easily stood out from the rest. He, like Brian, was seventeen. Later that day, Brian learned that Milton had already completed his schooling upon graduating from the eighth grade.

After the team competitions in tug-of-war were completed, each group selected an individual player to go one-on-one with the other competitors. After Milton easily defeated Prairie Grove's strongest player, Brian knew he wanted Milton on his football team, playing the O-line, protecting his blind side from hungry defensive players who lived to feast on quarterbacks.

Later at Frontier Days, during a three-on-three basketball tournament, Brian learned that Milton was quick on his feet. After Milton blocked a shot of Brian's at the rim, the senior quarterback started recruiting. It was too late for the coming football season and Milton wasn't even in high school, but Brian was thinking college. Milton was that good.

"Do you like football?" asked Brian.

"I don't know. I've never been to a game before," Milton responded.

"Well, I'm inviting you," Brian promised.

"Sir," the waitress said, "would you like to order now?"

"Oh, sorry," Brian answered, "I'm waiting on an old friend."

"Have you been here before?" asked the waitress, dressed in Amish garb, a modest purple dress, her long brown hair hidden below her starched white prayer cap.

Brian considered the name of the restaurant, "Amanda's Amish Kitchen." The first time he'd heard the name he thought it was owned and run by the Amish. Later, he learned that the kitchen's cuisine was Amish, but the restaurant had English, not Amish, owners. "At least some of the local Amish girls had employment close to their homes, and they, no doubt, earned generous tips from the tourists," thought Brian.

"I get here once every year or two, so I never get tired of your delicious food. I smelled the bread from outside."

"It's fresh all day; pies too," answered the waitress."

"I'd like to start with some bread and honey," said Brian, "but I can't decide between the chicken and dumplings, or the meatloaf. Are they both available?"

"Yes, and today we also have corn meal mush as well as butter noodles. Both are popular with our customers."

"Oh, no, more good choices!" said Brian, in mocked distress. "Good thing I have a few more minutes to decide. I'm early for our meeting."

Brian watched the teenage waitress glance at the book he had brought with him; it was lying on the table.

"What's your name?" asked Brian.

"Rebecca," she replied.

"Are you a student when you're not working here?"

"No, I'm out of school."

"High school?" asked Brian, already knowing the answer.

"No, elementary school. We Amish don't go past the eighth grade with formal education."

"Is that true for everyone?" Brian inquired.

"Every Amish I know," said Rebecca.

"My wife says I ask too many questions. Thanks for putting up with me."

"It's okay, I'm used to questions, but I don't always have the right answers."

"Nice to meet you. I'm Brian McDonald. I used to attend college in Wichita. This is a yearbook from 1986, called *Parnassus*. It's got photographs of the students, teachers, and activities. Whenever I look at it, it brings back good memories."

Brian, smiling, reached for the yearbook, its binding loose. It popped open to a well-worn page. "That's me, number one, throwing a long pass," he said. "I was the starting quarterback and had a strong arm back then." As he mentioned his arm, he lifted it and rotated his shoulder, checking its range of motion.

Rebecca looked at the black and white photo, then glanced at other pictures on both pages.

"I'll bet photographs do cause a person to think back to when they were young," said Rebecca as she considered recent photographs of her taken at an Amish pasture party. She had them hidden under her bedroom dresser drawer.

"I'll be back with your warm bread and honey," promised Rebecca, as she welcomed new arrivals and invited them to sit at a nearby table.

Brian again gazed out the window. He remembered Humble's Frontier Days and many of the activities during that long, hot August day so many years ago. He didn't recall the parade, pig races, or buggy races, but he remembered the tug-of-war contest, basketball, and the three-legged sack race when he and Milton had teamed up to win in the category for young adults.

The three-legged race was the first, not the last time, the two athletes played together competitively.

Rebecca approached with her customer's order and pitcher of water. She asked, "May I refill your glass?"

"Yes, thank you," replied Brian as he slid the glass toward Rebecca.

"Where do you live now?" she inquired.

"Chicago, Illinois."

"I'd be lost if I ever visited that city!"

"Sometimes I get turned around, but I can usually find my way with my car's help or my phone. I'm used to city driving now, but there's way too much traffic. You have it made here. No traffic jams."

"During our Frontier Days, the town is packed together like an Amish wedding," said a grinning Rebecca, a term she had no doubt used before.

"Does your family farm?" asked Brian.

"Yes, we dairy farm."

"I hear that's demanding work with long hours. Is that right?"

"Yes, its long hours but we're used to it. My father says it's better than having to work off the farm for someone else."

Suddenly, Rebecca watched as her customer's eyes lit up. His mouth broadened into a wide smile. Someone special, someone Mr. McDonald admired, had just entered the front door. Moving his chair backward, he prepared to stand.

Curious, Rebecca turned her head so she could see the person her customer called a friend.

"Brian!" said the Amish man.

"Jersey!" the English customer replied.

"Dad!" Rebecca squeaked.

# 15

# Deputy Jennings
# Digs Deeper

Tom Jennings was on his computer a lot and he wasn't playing games. He was learning about the Amish.

Tom read documents answering the standard questions about the Old Order Amish:

- "Where do the Amish live?"
- "Why are they against technology?"
- "Why do they dress that way?"
- "Are they non-violent?"
- "What is the role of women in their culture?"
- "Are the young people leaving the Amish family and community or staying?"

Compared to the heavy concentration of Old Order Amish in the states of Ohio, Pennsylvania, and Indiana, the Amish who Tom met near Humble in Cottonwood County were part of a settlement represented by only two church districts. Kansas had a population of approximately 1,500 total Amish, including children.

Since Tom had grown up with the convenience of technology, he couldn't imagine coping without electricity, especially his phone. He was so spoiled he didn't know it. When there was an emergency, he didn't give a second thought to responding in his department's marked SUV at speeds requiring strobe lights and a blaring siren. It was beyond his imagination to use a horse for transportation. But if he had a horse, as big as he was, it would require a reinforced stepladder or a loading dock for him to mount.

Tom learned that Amish traditions and rules could make things inconvenient, but the reasoning to the Plain People was clear. To keep a strong family, community, and faith, being separate from the modern world was preferred, and obedience to the church's teachings a necessity.

Tom understood why the Amish wouldn't accept him. The Amish and English really did live in separate worlds. For Tom, finding an Amish friend could develop into a fulfilling personal and cultural relationship. But for the Amish, he represented a potential threat to a way of life, an outsider who could eventually pull members away from their core values and ethnic identity. That, Tom speculated, was one of the reasons the Old Order Amish didn't believe in missionary work. Being a missionary would expose a Plain Person to a modern world that could contaminate their Amish thinking and lead to rejection of over four hundred years of tradition. It just wasn't worth the risk. It was a matter of religious survival.

Amish had an identity protected by rules, including standards about what and what was not permitted regarding clothing, grooming, transportation, education, and employment. To what degree the Amish cooperated with governmental authorities was also an issue.

For a moment, Tom considered his identity as a peace officer. Was he part of a closed group? Cops were distinct with similar customs and traditions. They wore uniforms and drove recognizable vehicles. They carried guns, and when necessary, shot and killed people. On the police radio they used their own ten-code language. Most of all, they identified as being a police family with common traits and goals, especially the belief that their purpose was to serve and protect humanity. This meant respecting and protecting the innocent from deception, oppression, and intimidation. In the line of duty, police officers were prepared to make the ultimate sacrifice so that citizens could continue to enjoy liberty, equality, and justice.

Until Tom started researching the Amish, he hadn't realized their extensive history of being persecuted. He knew that many groups had emigrated from Europe due to religious persecution, he just never pictured the Amish in the same boat with Puritans or Quakers. He learned that in 1737, the first Amish group made an extremely dangerous journey to the United States when they sailed on the ship *Charming Nancy,* later referred to as the "Amish Mayflower."

At first, Tom thought Anabaptists were against baptism. He couldn't have been further from the truth. Anabaptists rejected infant baptism because they believed scripture: the choice of following Jesus should be a voluntary one.

After reading about the persecution of the Amish in Europe, Tom's respect for the group grew. When the Amish chose to separate their religion from the state, that decision created powerful enemies for them. Amish persecution by government entities was barbaric. Many were burned at the stake or decapitated, others imprisoned and tortured. The extreme government response to a non-violent group showed how much the growth of independent "radical" groups was feared by those in control.

Like Quakers, the Amish were nonviolent, peace-loving people. In the face of persecution, they chose to emigrate, not fight.

No wonder the Amish had learned to circle their wagons—or buggies—to keep their tightly-knit community closed to outsiders.

It seemed to Tom that the United States was an ideal landing spot for larger groups of Amish. Beginning in the mid-1700s, they mostly settled and stayed. Despite intermittent prejudicial encounters, the agricultural Amish became well-respected far and wide for being good neighbors who were devout, industrious, law-abiding, and fair-minded.

As the world became more modern, especially during the Industrial Revolution, many Amish did leave their church and joined various Mennonite groups. But the Amish who held to their customs, like those in Cottonwood County, remained easily identifiable as Old Order Amish.

Tom considered the Yoders and the Schrocks. They were excellent representatives of the Amish—distinct and separate people—who, he accepted, wouldn't become his close friends but would always be friendly.

For a moment, Tom wondered if the Yoders or Schrocks would ever trust him enough to contact him if their community were being attacked or threatened by bullies or criminals. He had read stories online of how Amish were sometimes the target of discrimination or harassment because of being different, but he had never known it to occur in Cottonwood County. He decided it was time for him to ask.

The internet told of offenses against the Amish that included verbal harassment, criminal damage to property, theft of property, and injury because of objects being thrown at them when they were pedestrians or while riding in their buggies. One infant had even died in her mother's arms when a heavy tile was thrown into a buggy by high school age boys out having "fun." This was unacceptable to Tom. He felt a strong calling to be the Amish police or at least their guardian.

In Tom's opinion, the days of Amish persecution should have ended centuries earlier. It wasn't clear to him if the Amish welcomed persecution or just accepted it as a consequence of being different. Did acts of persecution make the Amish community stronger? If he could catch a person throwing rocks from a fast-moving car at a horse-and-buggy, he'd respond without hesitation. Even though the Plain People might not request a deputy, and they probably wouldn't cooperate as victims, how could he ignore a criminal offense? Tom still needed to figure out if his enforcement of a law was in any way perceived as disrespectful to the Amish. Was it okay for him to do his duty if he weren't requested to help? He surely didn't want to put anyone in a position of being excommunicated or shunned because of his response to a possible hate crime.

Tom had an idea. The county had a restorative justice program called Victim Offender and Reconciliation Program (VORP). Its goal was to allow offenders and victims an opportunity to meet face-to-face so that each party could better understand the offense and its impact. Tom thought this might be acceptable to Amish leaders because the program focused on recognizing the injustice or violation, not on the authorities punishing the offender.

Would the mixing of cultures be forbidden because it was too personally interactive with English outsiders? Only time would tell. The Amish were in no hurry.

# 16

## Final Chapter
## Deputy Jennings Tells a Story

Deputy Tom Jennings and Yackel pulled into Adam and Rosanna Yoder's driveway with the latest news. The German shepherd was in the backseat with the rear windows slightly down, his nose pressed to the vented window. Yackel von Baerenzwinger either recognized the farmstead or a familiar scent.

Two children playing in front of the house spotted the patrol car and ran inside to safety. Seconds later, their father, Adam, opened the front door as he was putting on his straw hat. He walked towards the vehicle with the sheriff's star on the door as Jennings considered the oppressive summer heat.

"Hello, Adam, good to see you again," greeted Jennings through the car's open window as the air conditioning struggled to cool the interior.

"Likewise, Officer Jennings," said Adam, as he waited to learn if the deputy was a bearer of unwelcome news.

"I've got some information to share," said Jennings, "all good, I think."

Adam waited.

Rosanna approached the car, carrying her youngest.

"Hello, Rosanna," said Jennings. "It's been a while."

"Deputy Jennings was telling me he's got some news to share with us," said Adam.

"We always like good news," offered Rosanna, watching Jennings' face for a clue as to what kind of information he had for them. "Would you like a glass of water or tea? It's been a long muggy day."

"That's nice of you," said Jennings, as he released his seat belt.

Yackel whimpered loudly.

Rosanna touched her cheek.

Jennings spoke to his four-legged partner. "Yackel, calm down, everything's okay."

Yackel scratched at the window with a paw, whimpered again, and sniffed the outside air. He stared at Rosanna holding her child.

"It will be cooler for us if we sit outside in the shade," said Adam.

Rosanna handed over the child to her husband and walked towards the house.

Perspiring heavily, Jennings escaped his tangled seat belt, but left the engine on so the air conditioning would keep Yackel safe from overheating.

"If you can chain your dog up, then he's invited to sit outside with us. No need to keep your car's motor running," said Adam. "Rosanna has had a fear of German shepherds ever since she was bitten by one as a child, but our children have about convinced her that we need a dog as a pet. I told them that if we must feed a dog then the dog will have to work for his room and board."

"Yackel sure earns his keep," said Jennings, "although, when he finds illegal drugs for us, he thinks it's a game. He just wants to play with his ball."

"Here she comes now," said Adam.

"I'll get Yackel if you're sure it's all right. I'd hate for him to frighten her."

Before Jennings had moved, Rosanna arrived with glasses of tea.

"Rosanna, Deputy Jennings was about to get his dog from the car and show him to me. Is that acceptable to you?"

As Rosanna sat down, she thought about the day so long ago when she had been viciously bitten in her face, leaving her with a life-long scar. "Will he be tied up?" she asked.

"I'll have him on his leash. He's trained to obey me," replied Jennings. "If I tell him to sit, he'll sit. If I tell him to stay, he'll stay."

"Yes, okay, I think I'm overdue for socializing with German shepherds. It's been too long. Does he speak Pennsylvania Dutch?" asked a nervous but smiling Rosanna.

"I don't know about your dialect, but he knows basic commands in German. If he follows any of your orders, then he needs to go back to K-9 school. He's been trained to only obey me and to only take food or treats from me."

When Jennings returned with Yackel, the K-9 was straining on his line, pulling his handler towards the Yoders. Excitedly, he started barking.

Jennings yanked on his leash and yelled, "*NEIN*! Yackel, NO!"

Adam, holding his baby girl, instinctively stood up to protect her and Rosanna. His wife remained sitting, staring at the dog, then holding both hands in front of her face like a shield.

Finally, Yackel responded to his handler, gradually calming down.

"*SITZ*!" yelled Jennings.

"Sorry about that," Jennings apologized. "I have an idea about what got into him."

Adam remained standing. He was silent, but Rosanna spoke up. "I guess I'm not as ready as I thought I was to have another dog. He gave me a scare."

Changing the subject, Rosanna asked Jennings, "Did you say you have good news to share?"

"I'm not sure if this is good or bad news, but I wanted you to be the first one I told outside of law enforcement. You remember my investigation a month ago when we first met?"

"Of course!" she laughed, relaxing. "Thanks for not taking me to jail! Although it would have given me a break from all the housework. Do the jailers permit knitting needles in the cells or are they considered deadly weapons?"

"I'll check on that if and when you're arrested," replied Jennings as the ends of his lips displayed a soft smile. "When I was here, I thought I was going to have my military mustache shaved off by a gang of angry Amish," joked Jennings. "Those black buggies just kept coming! I thought I was a goner!"

Chuckling, both Rosanna and Adam enjoyed his exaggeration.

"Well," continued the deputy, "Harley Beasley, the guy who called 911 about you allegedly stealing dirt from your ditch was arrested earlier today by our detectives."

"What for?" asked Adam.

"For theft of county property."

"What did he steal?" asked a curious Rosanna.

"County dirt, topsoil," said Jennings, waiting for a look of bewilderment from both Rosanna and Adam.

He didn't have to wait long before Rosanna, her head cocked, inquired, "County dirt from a county ditch?"

"Basically, yes. Awhile back his wife caught him cheating on her, hired an attorney, and filed for an emergency divorce. The attorney contacted our department with information about an ongoing criminal enterprise. Harley's wife was aware that her husband, who drove truck for the Road and Bridge Department, had been stealing topsoil for years and using it in his landscaping business. The attorney's offering his client's testimony as a cooperating witness with an expectation that she won't be charged or do any time."

"That's unfortunate about Mr. Beasley," said Rosanna.

"Yes, we cannot rejoice but we can ask God to help him find his way," said Adam.

Jennings could have guessed that the Yoders wouldn't use his news as an opportunity to gloat or to find satisfaction with another person's failings. Milton and Irene Schrock had already demonstrated to Tom the Amish ability to quickly forgive others. Shawn Harris had nearly killed their twins, Reuben and Rebecca, when he drove his truck into their horse-and-wagon, yet they had forgiven Harris before the dead equine could attract blow flies.

"I have more news," said Jennings. "I never thought that Harley Beasley would break the law, but what I found out yesterday is just unbelievable! I've been reading Amish history and I've learned a lot. One book is about the origins of the Amish religion and about the Anabaptists and how you believe in adult baptism, and about the history of persecution your people have encountered, beginning in Europe."

Adam and Rosanna glanced at one another. "This ought to be interesting," thought Rosanna, "an English deputy's going to interpret our Amish history!" Adam tried not to laugh; if he waited long enough everyone was an expert on the Amish. Amused, Adam imagined

English Jennings giving the Sunday sermon while wearing his deputy uniform with a loaded gun on his belt. No, it wasn't going to happen.

"I read about a document that was drafted," stated Jennings. "It focused on being obedient children of God, separated from the world, and completely at peace. And the book mentioned the town of Schleitheim at the Swiss-German border."

"Yes, Schleitheim," repeated Adam. "Surely, he hasn't read *Martyrs' Mirror*," he thought.

Jennings continued, "The name of the town looked familiar to me even though I've never been to Europe or studied European history."

With his pocket handkerchief, Jennings wiped perspiration from his face and bald head as he watched Rosanna and Adam. They waited for him to make his point. He also observed Yackel. The canine hadn't taken his eyes off Rosanna. Then, catching a movement at the window of the house, Tom counted the faces of three inquisitive children.

"Yesterday morning, after working all night, I couldn't get to sleep," said Jennings. "Then I finally remembered where I'd heard of Schleitheim. I got up and reviewed the file I have on Yackel. That's when I re-examined his certification papers. He was born and trained in Schleitheim!"

"Amazing!" said Adam, leaning forward.

"Small world," said Rosanna, while watching Yackel.

"I contacted the owner of the certified dog training business in Switzerland. His name is Peter Borntrager."

Knowing that Borntrager was Rosanna's maiden name, Tom stopped and waited.

"Borntrager?" asked Rosanna, while staring at the big deputy.

"Yes," replied Jennings.

"Adam," said Rosanna, "I thought there was no trace of any Borntragers left in Switzerland or Germany. I thought everyone had emigrated."

"That's been my understanding," replied Adam, "at least the Amish Borntragers."

Jennings reached into one of the deep and wide pockets on his duty pants and pulled out a folded paper. "I've copied off my brief correspondence with Peter for you to have in case you wish to contact him. He said his grandfather's Amish settlement in Germany ended in 1937 and merged with a local Mennonite congregation."

"Did he mention the name of his grandfather?" asked Rosanna.

"Let me see," said Jennings as he studied his notes. "Here it is, John E. Borntrager."

Rosanna let out a yelp, "Oh!"

Yackel stood up, on guard.

"Peter trained Yackel?" she asked, seeking confirmation.

"Yes," said Jennings, "that's what he told me. Said his family has trained dogs going back centuries to the days when they were shepherds near the . . ." Again, Jennings examined his notes and said, "Schwarzbach River."

"Yackel, come here boy!" said Rosanna, clapping her hands as she encouraged personal contact.

Yackel turned his head and checked with his handler.

Tom approved and dropped the leash.

"Come here Yackel" ordered Rosanna. "Give your cousin a kiss!"

Yackel approached Rosanna cautiously, confused that he was being allowed, even encouraged, to get closer. He lifted his nose and again sniffed the air. He turned his head one more time and made eye contact with Tom. He had permission.

Rosanna got off her chair and kneeled on the ground. "Come over here and say hello!"

Finally, Yackel transformed from an on-duty police dog to an excited pup. He may have recognized the woman's accent or tone of voice from his upbringing in Switzerland. Somehow, he had confirmed the Borntrager family scent faster than DNA matching in a data base.

To Yackel, Peter and Rosanna were one. He hurried to the woman's outstretched arms.

Hugging the German shepherd, Rosanna began to cry.

With a feeling of family familiarity, Yackel licked Rosanna's scar and her cascading tears.

Rosanna closed her eyes. She bowed her head and thanked God. Tears of happiness, bottled up since childhood, set her free.

jimpotterauthor.com

sandhenge
PUBLICATIONS

# About the Author

## Frequently Asked Questions

Photo by Shelley Stephens

## 1. Is this story about Deputy Jennings meeting the Amish, based on a true story?

No, but it's based on a career in law enforcement, including my years working as a patrol officer, school resource officer, and civil process server. I consider Tom Jennings my alter ego, which means there's a little of me in the fictional character. I've also had the good fortune to know people of the Amish faith. Certainly, the idea that landowners recovering their garden's topsoil from a county ditch would be charged with a crime, is ridiculous. Yet, that's where I started the story.

**2. You said in the preface of the book that the idea for this story came from a comment from a friend.**

Yes, when the conditions are ideal, seeds grow overnight. My friend wondered where the county was taking the soil that had eroded into the ditch near her house. It wasn't long before Deputy Tom Jennings, a fictional character from my earlier novel, *Taking Back the Bullet*, made an encore. Soon, the big deputy, a K-9 officer, drove his patrol car into the story to investigate.

**3. When you started writing this book, did you know the ending?**

There are two vastly distinct kinds of writers, one plans and plots, the other type just starts writing and discovers the story along the way. As you can imagine, many writers fall somewhere in between these two broad categories.

I began writing *Deputy Jennings Meets the Amish* without creating an outline or knowing the ending. It was a leap of faith for me because normally I have a story completed before posting. However, in this case, I wrote and posted a chapter each week before figuring out what would happen the following week.

On the other hand, with *Taking Back the Bullet: Trajectories of Self-Discovery*, I did an incredible amount of research and plotting prior to writing. I still laugh out loud when I recall planning the bank robbery down to its smallest detail. Every time I had personal business at my brick-and-mortar bank in Hutchinson (Kansas) I avoided the drive-through. Instead, I entered the bank so I could scope out the surveillance cameras, imagine the response of the bank tellers to a hold-up, and smell the gunpowder and pooled blood after the fictional shoot-out. If the employees only knew what I was thinking!

### 4. What caused you to have Deputy Jennings return as a central character to *Deputy Jennings Meets the Amish*?

Already knowing one of my fictional characters at the beginning of the process gave me a foot in the door to this make-believe, though realistic, world. As a law enforcement officer, Jennings had a legitimate reason to interact with a culture foreign to him. Despite his position of authority, Jennings could display his ignorance about the Old Order Amish in a non-threatening way.

I've met interesting fictional people. Occasionally, writers must deal with unruly or demanding characters. They may refuse to be pawns in the story. If they try to take over and demand a larger role—more stage time— writers have a few options: welcome them, ignore them, or try and change them. I offer the assertive characters lines to see if they can pass the audition.

**5. In *Taking Back the Bullet* you have a diverse group of characters.**

I asked the question, "What happens when you put an obese police officer, a person with a mental illness, and a Native American girl with albinism, all in the same book?" They all meet in Prairie Grove, Kansas, during a botched bank robbery. Due to a single bullet, their lives are changed forever.

The characters are stigmatized, but once they discover their true identities, each is empowered to begin the journey of life's purpose.

**6. The characters are flawed, yet welcoming.**

The novel is a reminder to us all to stop being so judgmental of others; to give people a break. One inadvertent action can unknowingly change the lives of so many people. Our world is complex, and we're all connected. We do the best we can do under the circumstances, yet, we still have the potential to change and make a difference.

**7. In the novel, *Taking Back the Bullet*, you write extensively about Native Americans and life on the reservation. Is this part of your background?**

I don't know of any personal Native American connections in my family history. As a child growing up, I do recall the positive impression I had of reading about Nez Perce Chief Joseph's incredible efforts when he and his people attempted to flee from the United States Army to Canada in 1877. In planning my novel, after learning that Chief Joseph was buried on the Colville Confederated Tribes Reservation in the state of Washington, I knew where my fictional characters would call home. To better learn the backstory of my Native American characters, I visited the reservation, especially Chief Joseph's grave.

### 8. Since you had a career in law enforcement, do you have ideas for more stories?

My law enforcement career gave me the opportunity to meet a wide spectrum of people, especially during their most stressful moments. *Cop in the Classroom: Lessons I've Learned, Tales I've Told*, is my police memoir.

The book's structure is based on me answering questions from kids who knew me as a deputy. They asked:

- "Is your gun loaded?"
- "Can I try on your handcuffs?"
- "Have you ever arrested a drunk driver?"
- "Have you ever watched anyone die?"

But it's also about me using my stressful encounters from my patrol officer days to help encourage kids to make good decisions. My experiences of arresting adults and watching others die gave me the impetus to dedicate myself to help save young lives.

By establishing personal relationships with my students and using my true-life stories as examples of what happens when people make poor choices, I helped children understand how personal decisions effect outcomes.

### 9. People often want to know the habits of writers. Do you have a specific routine when you write?

I understand that not everyone is a "morning person," but I've developed a writing routine that serves me well. I'm usually up by 6 a.m. working on my research and writing. Before I retired, I started at 5 a.m. because I was motivated to do my writing before I went to work for someone else.

I write first thing because that's before interruptions. It's also when my creative juices have been trained to produce; they urge me to get the ideas into words on my computer screen. Later, I edit. That's fun, too.

A writing routine can be very productive; however, bad habits waste time and energy. Lately, I've started checking and answering emails before I write my stories. Then I'll peek at the news. If I'm not careful, I've squandered my best writing time.

When I have a writing idea, I'm quick to jot it down on the closest piece of paper. Rarely do I reach for my phone. My best ideas come to me when I'm outside taking a walk or gardening, while I'm taking a shower, or when I wake up during the night. Occasionally, after a restless night, I'll look at my bedside table notes and try to decipher my handwriting.

### 10. **Did you always want to be a writer?**

No. As a child I wanted to be the Lone Ranger, on my horse named Silver, fighting outlaws in the Old West with Tonto, my trusted companion. Superman, who fought for truth, justice, and the American way, was another hero of mine.

You could call me a "late bloomer" when it comes to writing. I didn't attend college to become a writer, but my classes, especially my graduate school degrees, taught me the joys of research and composing. My MA in history included a thesis on an Illinois Civil War Regiment. Research meant studying the regiment's original muster roll located in Springfield, Illinois. A trip to the National Archives in Washington, D.C. allowed me to read the pension records of "my" men. While I was focused on nonfiction, the work required me to use my imagination, to tell stories, and to learn the rules of writing.

In my opinion today, anyone who has written a college thesis certainly qualifies as a writer.

### 11. **When did you *know* you were a writer?**

I wrote a short play, *Under the Radar: Race at School.* It was awarded a fellowship for playwriting by the

Kansas Arts Commission and the National Endowment of the Arts.

Over a long weekend, while preparing for a workshop I was leading about exploring and valuing diversity, an idea struck me. I wanted to find a way to personally involve workshop attendees in a fictional racist encounter at a high school. The play, read in a group setting with fourteen characters, became an effective tool that guaranteed participation while encouraging an examination of different mind-sets.

### 12. **What advice would you give to a person who wants to become a writer, journalist, or author?**

It takes inspiration, imagination, and dedication.

Read, read, read. Write, write, write. Do both. Write a book review. Whether the genre is your favorite or one you typically avoid, you learn a great deal from reading books. Interview someone. Take a walk. Travel. Keep a journal. Write a poem.

Memories make memoirs. People write memoirs for many reasons: a personal need, for others, to understand or heal, to remember, to be remembered, or to forget. Here's good news: memoir doesn't normally require a lot of research, you already know the characters, setting, and even the dialogue.

Everyone will find their own path. For me, it was going to college and later becoming a peace officer. Working in law enforcement as a patrol officer gave me valuable experience in the "real" world.

To solve or explain an event, officers must learn the importance of close observation, and be able to ask and answer the five W's (who, what, where, when, why) and how. They interview people. Not only do officers meet many interesting characters, but they write multiple reports every shift with an immediate, real deadline. They can't go home until the work is completed.

Deadlines—artificial or real—make all the difference. In school and at work, every assignment has a deadline. For years I posted a blog every Wednesday morning. Now I've shifted my priorities to bigger writing projects where I don't want to be interrupted by a weekly blog.

The sooner you start your journey, the sooner you'll arrive at your destination.

### 13. You're an active member of the Kansas Authors Club. What have you gained from your membership?

The Kansas Authors Club is rewarding because of the opportunities to meet all kinds of writers, to learn their creative craft, and to help and be helped by others. Now I have more writer friends.

Some members and guests enjoy the meetings with speakers while others prefer the gatherings where they have an opportunity to share their literary work.

If you're interested in writing, I encourage you to find others who will be supportive of your journey. There are local groups and online gatherings. The Kansas Authors Club holds monthly meetings in person and virtually, plus it holds an annual convention. If you're looking for support or advice on your writing, check out the Kansas Authors Club's (KAC) website at kansasauthorsclub.org or kansasauthors.org.

### 14. Are your books available on your website and in bookstores?

My award-winning website has a lot of information about my books and writing, especially from years of weekly blogs/podcasts. You can explore this at jimpotterauthor.com. My books are also available at bookstores all around the country, and at amazon.com. I may be contacted at jim@copintheclassroom.com and 620-899-3144. I also have a Facebook page.

### 15. What writing project are you working on now?

I'm obsessed with learning as much as possible about Charles Collins, the first sheriff of Reno County. I know that his grandfather immigrated from Ireland prior to 1800 and settled near Baton Rouge, Louisiana. I'm still looking for the location of the Collins plantation and relatives—ancestors and descendants. Besides working on his biography, I have stories written on all the other Reno County sheriffs (including the real Tom Jennings), beginning with Collins, elected in 1872.

## 16. What have we missed? What would you like for people to know about you and your writing?

Writers are fortunate to have one person believe in them. I have Alex, my trusted and talented wife as first reader of my books. She's also an exceptional artist who has created sculptures for many of my fictional characters in *Taking Back the Bullet*. The photographs are included in the novel.

Thanks for reading *Deputy Jennings Meets the Amish*.

Until we meet virtually or in person, happy writing and reading.

*Jim*

UNDER
THE
RADAR
RACE AT SCHOOL
a *short* play

JIM POTTER

*Under the Radar: Race at School* is a short play. It examines the narrow and broad effects that come from the cultural and social lives of a group of high school students and their extended, mostly white community. Each character brings his and her unique point of view and reaction to a confrontation between two of the school's students.

The play is targeted for a secondary-adult age level and is useful as a teaching tool. A discussion guide follows the text of the play.

# COP IN THE CLASSROOM

## Lessons I've Learned, Tales I've Told

### SGT. JIM POTTER

Learn how kids and cops connect at school. You will enjoy 33 personal stories about one officer's professional career as a deputy sheriff and school resource officer. *Cop in the Classroom,* a police memoir, gives an insider's look at the emotional experiences behind the badge—and life lessons for us all.

This contemporary, character-driven novel is about
people who are stigmatized. However, once they
discover their true identities, each is empowered to
begin the journey of life's purpose.

The main characters are police officer Tom Jennings,
obese as a mutant Idaho potato in a jiggling gelatin suit;
James Odessa-Smith, with his schizoaffective disorder;
and young Suanna Morningcloud, a person with
albinism, half Nez Perce Indian and half Caucasian.

Meeting during a botched bank robbery in Prairie
Grove, Kansas, they experience tragedy and trauma.
Forever changed and connected, they are forced to ask,
"Who am I and where do I belong?"

*Taking Back the Bullet* explores the themes of stigma,
identity, and self-discovery. The multi-layered stories
are an escape into reality.

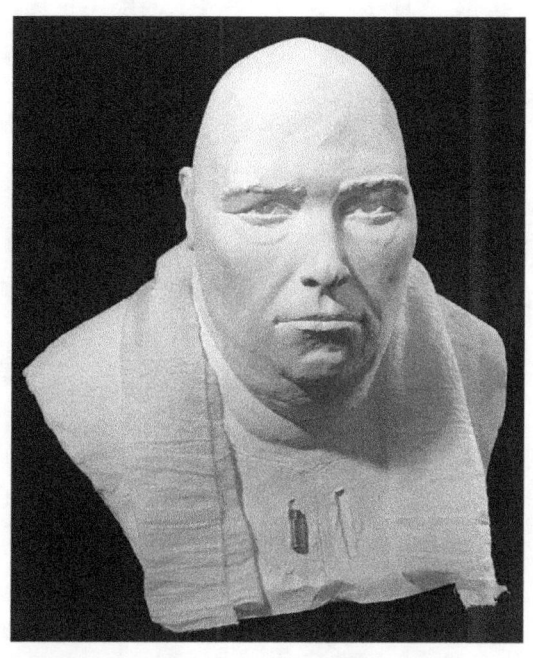

*Tom Jennings*, a sculpture created by J. Alex Potter,
represents the main fictional character in
*Taking Back the Bullet*.

Photograph by Gina Laiso.

J. Alex Potter sculpted the fictional characters found in
*Taking Back the Bullet: Trajectories of Self-Discovery.*

Photograph by Gina Laiso.

www.ingramcontent.com/pod-product-compliance
Lightning Source LLC
Chambersburg PA
CBHW070329120726
47909CB00008B/2653